Once upon a Poodle

By Chrysa Smith

Illustrated by Pat Achilles

Published by The Well Bred Book

No matter how young or old we are, we are always learning.

In this story about one little dog, he learns many of the same things we do. He learns about the love of a mother; the comfort of family. What it feels like to be bored or different or alone. Or sometimes, the feeling that what is going on at this very moment will always be the same.

This story is also about hope---knowing that things always change. When we feel bad or different or alone, it is important to remember that we will not always feel that way. My mother always told me, *"You never know what life has waiting for you just around the corner."*

So keep walking and hopping and skipping--and watch out for those corners. They come when you least expect them.

Happy Tales,
Chrysa Smith

One afternoon, a little poodle named Woody sat upon the sofa and watched the world from the window.

He saw birds soaring through the sky. He saw squirrels climbing up trees. He saw rabbits hopping. And he saw groups of dogs running and playing together.

His mom, Mrs. Flout, played games with him; games like Hide-the-Bone, but she wasn't terribly good at it.

When Woody hid the bone in her slipper, she looked under the pillow. When he hid it under the pillow, she looked inside her slippers.

Woody loved his mom as much as a poodle could. But what he really longed for was a brother. Someone who played Hide-the-Bone just a bit better. Someone to keep him company when Mrs. Flout was busy. And someone who could be part of the family.

So one day, Woody got to thinking that if he wanted to solve his problem, he needed to be on the other side of the window. He needed to be where everyone else seemed to be.

While Mrs. Flout was busy taking a bubble bath that brimmed over the tub, Woody popped out through the tiny dog door where he met a fellow with a long neck and feathers.

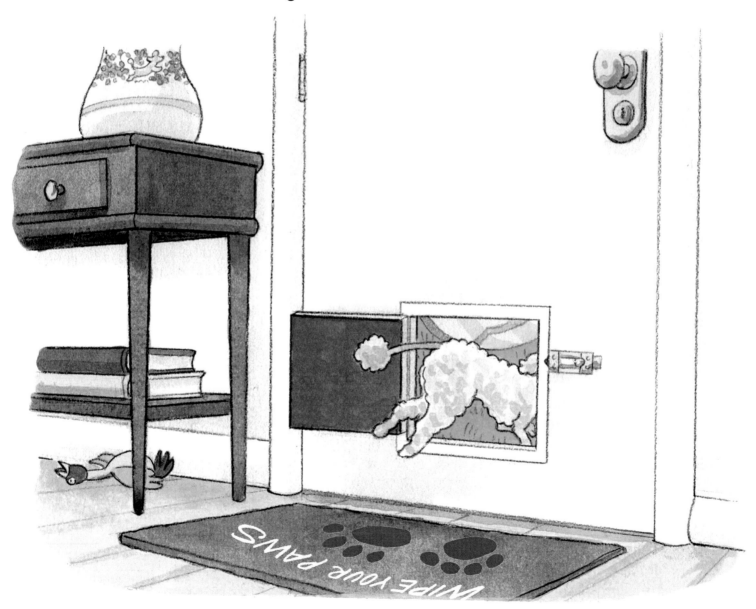

They sniffed each other and the mysterious creature shook his tail feathers. Woody was sure that meant he wanted to play, so Woody chased him all the way up the path, through the dog door and into the house.

Could this be the one? Woody wondered. *Could this be my new brother?* So he threw over one of his bouncy balls. But the creature just stood there and flapped his wings. So Woody threw a stuffed bird to him, and he let out a screeching squawk. The winged creature took off, flying through the Flout house, down the hall and straight into the bathroom.

Plop. He landed right in the bathtub, face-to-face with Mrs. Flout.

"Oh my!" sang Mrs. Flout. "Where in the world did you come from? We must return you to where you belong. You need to be near water, but not in my tub."

Woody was sad that the big bird couldn't stay. So the next day, he went back to his sofa and watched the world through the window once again.

This time, Mrs. Flout was busy baking peanut butter bones. So Woody popped out through the dog door and ran into a furry gray fellow with a bushy tail.

He was chewing on a big nut and threw one toward Woody. *Hmm,* Woody thought, *this guy likes to play fetch.* So Woody and his friend threw the nut back and forth as they went up the path, through the dog door and into the house.

Could this be the one? Woody wondered. *Could this be my new brother?*

Woody threw over a stuffed squirrel toy that looked amazingly like this furry fellow. He let out a few squeaks that sounded like fighting birds. Then he jumped up on the kitchen table, ran across the counter —

— and leaped straight into Mrs. Flout's pile of nuts.

"Oh my!" squealed Mrs. Flout. "Where in the world did you come from? We must return you to where you belong. You need to gather nuts from trees, not my kitchen."

Woody was sad that the furry fellow couldn't stay. So the next day, he went back to his sofa and watched the world through his window again.

While Mrs. Flout was in the garden, Woody popped out of the dog door and ran into a floppy-eared guy with a small white tail. Woody threw him a little blue berry buried beneath some leaves. The floppy-eared guy sent it back with his nose. So Woody thought he wanted to play.

Could this be the one? Woody wondered. *Could this be my new brother?*

Woody led the little fellow up the path to the dog door, but when Woody got inside, there was no sign of the floppy-eared guy.

So he went back outside and found his new friend chomping through a pile of carrots as Mrs. Flout picked them.

"Oh my!" yelled Mrs. Flout; "Where in the world did you come from? We must return you to where you can hop and find your favorite food, but not my garden."

Woody was sad that the floppy-eared creature couldn't stay. So he went back to his sofa and watched the world through his window again.

While Mrs. Flout was busy bringing in packages from the car, Woody popped out through the dog door and down the path. But this time, something was different. A curly-haired black creature with four legs and a tail came running toward him. He chased Woody right through the dog door and into the house.

When Woody threw his furry dog toy, the creature brought it back. When Woody hid his bone, the creature sniffed it out.

Could this be the one? Woody thought. *Could this be my new brother?*

Mrs. Flout came in and said to the little pup, "I see you have a name tag, Archie, from the local animal shelter. You might need a good home. Would you like to stay and play awhile?"

Mrs. Flout called the shelter and was told that Archie had escaped through a hole in the fence. They were glad he was safe, and asked if she could bring him back.

Seeing how well he and Woody got along, Mrs. Flout cried, "Oh my! Must we return him? He seems like he is where he belongs, as part of our family. We would like to adopt him."

Woody barked with joy and thought, *THIS is the one! My new brother!*

Archie was lively, jumpy and cute. So he followed Woody to the sofa. But instead of watching the world through the window, Woody watched his brother Archie grab a bone and hide it somewhere in the sofa. Woody and Archie spent the next two hours playing Hide-the-Bone. Archie was much better at it than Mrs. Flout.

Mrs. Flout smiled at the two boys. Then she went and locked the dog door.

To find out more about Mrs. Flout, Woody, Archie and other new members of the family, step into the easy-reader series: The Adventures of the Poodle Posse.

Published by The Well Bred Book: **www.wellbredbook.net**

Chrysa Smith is a lifetime writer and author of the award-winning, easy-reader series called *The Adventures of the Poodle Posse. Once upon a Poodle* is her first picture book.

Pat Achilles is an illustrator for children's books, greeting cards and magazines. She especially likes drawing cute and funny animals like the Poodle Posse, and you can see more of her art and cartoons on her website www.achillesportfolio.com.

Laurel Garver is a Philadelphia-based editor who enjoys word games, Celtic music and quirky indie films. She is the author of two novels, *Never Gone* and *Almost There* and a poetry collection, *Muddy-Fingered Midnights*. She blogs at http://laurelgarver.blogspot.com.